DIGGING ARMADILLOS

by Judith Jango-Cohen

Lerner Publications Company • Minneapolis

Website address: www.lernerbooks.com

Curriculum Development Director: Nancy M. Campbell

Words in *italic type* are explained in a glossary
on page 30.

Library of Congress Cataloging-in-Publication Data

Jango-Cohen, Judith.
    Digging armadillos / Judith Jango-Cohen.
        p.   cm. — (Pull ahead books)
    Includes index.
    Summary: Introduces the physical characteristics,
behavior, and habitat of the nine-banded armadillo.
    ISBN 0-8225-3625-0 (hardcover : alk. paper).—
    ISBN 0-8225-3629-3 (pbk. : alk. paper)
    1. Nine-banded armadillo—Juvenile literature.
    [1. Nine-banded armadillo. 2. Armadillos.] I. Title.
    II. Series.
    QL737.E23J25 1999
    599.3'12—dc21   98–47482

Manufactured in the United States of America
1 2 3 4 5 6 – JR – 04 03 02 01 00 99

Why is this animal digging?

This is an armadillo.

Armadillos dig for many reasons.
Digging helps them stay alive.

SNIFF!
GRUNT!

This armadillo is smelling the ground. Do you know why?

Armadillos can smell bugs
under the ground.

They dig to find the bugs.

Then they lick up the bugs
with their long, sticky tongues.

SLURP!

Armadillos like bugs best,
but they eat plants, too.

Armadillos are *omnivores.*

Omnivores are animals that eat both plants and animals.

Are you an omnivore?

This armadillo is smelling the air
to find out if a *predator* is near.

A predator is an animal that hunts
and eats other animals.

Oh no! A dog is hunting nearby.
ZIP! The armadillo runs away.

What if it cannot run
faster than a predator?

The predator might try to bite.

A hard shell called a *carapace*
protects the armadillo's body.

How can an armadillo move
around in such a hard shell?

A carapace has many thin
bands in the middle.

Count the bands in the carapace
of this armadillo.

Bands help a carapace bend.

A carapace is heavy.
To escape from a predator,

an armadillo may need to swim.
How can it swim without sinking?

The armadillo swallows lots of air.
The air helps the armadillo float.

How else can armadillos
escape from predators?

They dig! SCRITCH-SCRATCH!

Quick as a flash, an armadillo
digs a small hole and hides inside.

Sharp claws
help an
armadillo
dig quickly.

An armadillo holds its breath as
it digs to keep dirt out of its nose.

An armadillo can also dig
a big hole called a *den.*

A den is a safe place
where an armadillo can rest.

A den also makes a cozy nest
for babies.

Armadillo babies are called *pups.*

A newborn pup can see and hear.
It has a soft pink carapace.

On the day it is born, a pup
can walk, climb, and play.

As it grows up, its carapace
will become hard and gray.

24

Armadillos belong to a group
of animals called *mammals.*

Like all baby mammals, armadillo
pups drink milk from their mother.

When pups are older, they leave their den to hunt for food.

Armadillos are amazing. They run, swim, hunt, grunt, sniff, and lick.

Most of all, they dig!

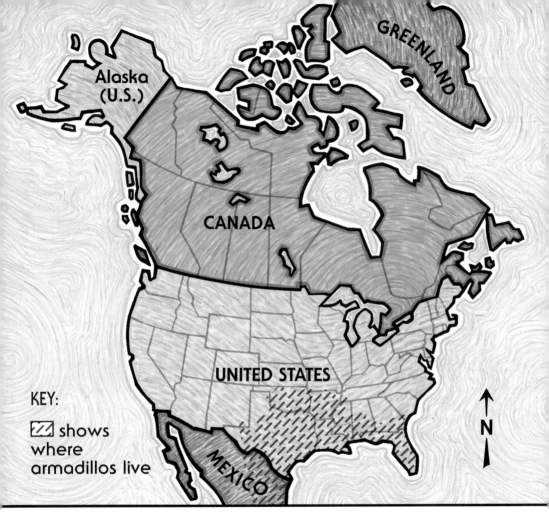

KEY:

▨ shows where armadillos live

Find your state or province on this map.
Do armadillos live near you?

Parts of an Armadillo's Body

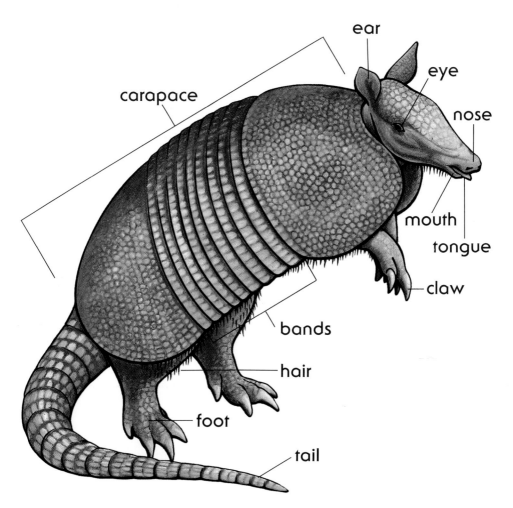

ear

eye

nose

carapace

mouth

tongue

claw

bands

hair

foot

tail

Glossary

carapace: the hard shell that covers the body of an armadillo

den: a cozy, safe place to live

mammals: animals that have hair and drink mother's milk when young. (Humans, wolves, bats, and whales are mammals.)

omnivores: animals that eat both plants and animals

predator: an animal that hunts and eats other animals

pups: baby armadillos

Hunt and Find

- **dens** of armadillos on pages 21, 26
- armadillos **digging** on pages 3, 6, 18, 20, 27
- armadillo **pups** on pages 22–25
- an armadillo **swimming** on page 17
- **tongues** of armadillos on pages 7, 9

The publisher wishes to extend special thanks to our **series consultant,** Sharyn Fenwick. An elementary science-math specialist, Mrs. Fenwick was the recipient of the National Science Teachers Association 1991 Distinguished Teaching Award. In 1992, representing the state of Minnesota at the elementary level, she received the Presidential Award for Excellence in Math and Science Teaching.

Eliot Cohen

About the Author

Judith Jango-Cohen grew up in a Boston apartment with cats, turtles, and tropical fish. She loved learning about plants and animals and got a degree in biology. For ten years she taught science to children. When her own children were born, she began working at her home in Burlington, Massachusetts, as a writer. With her husband, Eliot, and her children, Jennifer and Steven, Judith travels to many national parks. Observing the plants and animals there gives her ideas for magazine articles and books. Judith met her first armadillo on a trip to Florida.

Photo Acknowledgments

The photographs in this book are reproduced through the courtesy of: © Jim Dunlop, pages 12, 19; © Jeff Foott, front and back covers, pages 3, 4, 5, 6, 9, 10, 13, 14, 15, 16, 17, 18, 20, 21, 22, 23, 24, 25, 26, 27, 31; © Richard Goff, pages 7, 8; © D. Mutzbaugh, page 11.